Our Family Memories

Written and created by Judy Lawrence
© Copyright 1987, 1991, 1992, and 1995 by
Lawrence & Co. Publishers.

Printed in the United States of America

Cover illustration and graphic design by Amy Beyer

All rights reserved. No part of this book may be reproduced or transmitted in any form or by any means, electronic or mechanical, including photocopying, recording, or by any information storage and retrieval system without written permission from the author, except for the inclusion of brief quotations in a review.

Published by:

Blue Sky Marketing, Inc.
P.O. Box 21583-S
St. Paul, MN 55121
(612) 456-5602
SAN 263-9394

ISBN 0-911493-14-X

10   9   8   7   6   5

Introduction

Dear Friend,

Do the years and events seem to pass by so quickly that they suddenly become hazy memories? If so, then *Our Family Memories* will help you remember them. It is designed to complement photo albums, home movies, baby books, scrapbooks, grandparent books, and other keepsakes.

Keeping in mind your busy lifestyle, *Our Family Memories* is simple and efficient to use so you can organize and capture favorite memories forever. The format allows you to jot down a summary of what you did on any holiday or special occasion—just enough to jog your memory later on when you reminisce about life's special moments. If you received a special gift, gave an exceptional party, celebrated a 25th wedding anniversary, enjoyed a memorable reunion, or got together with old friends not seen in years, here is the place to record it all.

When you have completed the five-year record in *Our Family Memories*, you will have a storehouse of memories in a convenient, easy-to-review format and will have captured the spirit of the last five years instead of feeling as if these busy years have just passed by in a blur.

I hope you enjoy using this memory book as much as I enjoyed creating it.

—Judy Lawrence

Contents

Getting Started 6

Holidays
    New Year's Eve/Day 9
    Easter 14
    Memorial Day 16
    Independence Day 18
    Labor Day 20
    Thanksgiving 23
    Christmas Eve/Day 29
    (Note: Other holidays can be recorded under Special Celebrations)

Other Events
    Birthdays 41
    Guests & Visitors 49
    Milestones (Activities, Achievements, Events) 53
    Odds & Ends (Births, Current Events, etc.) 61
    Parties & Informal Gatherings 67
    Reunions 75
    Special Celebrations (Hanukkah, Mother's Day, etc.) 79
    Trips & Vacations 85
    Wedding Anniversaries 91

Extra Notes 94

Getting Started

Our Family Memories is designed to make it easy for you to recall the special events in your life. You can choose the amount of detail or summary information you wish to record.

While this book was designed for you to record the "highlights" of your experiences, some events may be particularly memorable and for that reason there are often Additional Remarks segments for you to expand into. Those segments may appear either within a section or at the end of a section or chapter.

Some holidays may, however, be no different than the average day. Rather than leave these pages blank, jot down a comment (e.g., "spent a quiet day at home working in the garden") just as a reminder for distinguishing the events of one year from another.

You can also decide what year you want to begin your records. It could be this year, your wedding year, or the year of a turning point in your life. If you remember the details from past years, start recording them today!

Our Family Memories is divided into two major sections:

> **Holidays** and
> **Other Events.**

Holidays is organized in chronological order and lets you record your holiday activities. There are special pages for

Getting Started

New Year's Eve/Day, Easter, Memorial Day, Independence Day, Labor Day, Thanksgiving, and Christmas Eve/Day. (Don't worry if you have other special celebrations you want to record such as Hanukkah, Passover, Valentine's Day, St. Patrick's Day, Mother's Day or Veteran's Day. There is space for them on the Special Celebrations pages in the second section!)

Within the Holidays section there is plenty of space for you to note Easter egg hunts, parades, fireworks, parties, and the people who were a part of your holiday celebrations.

Other Events is organized in alphabetical order and has pages for noting Birthdays, Guests & Visitors, Milestones, Odds & Ends, Parties & Informal Gatherings, Reunions, Special Celebrations, Trips & Vacations, and Wedding Anniversaries. These pages are ideal for summarizing and highlighting the various activities and accomplishments of your family.

Extra Notes is a page for your thoughts on events or subjects that you can't find a "home" for in another section.

Our Family Memories is designed to help you get started, but it is your own special memories that make this book a cherished treasure. Have fun!

New Year's Eve/Day

Happy New Year!

What a time to celebrate! Get out the party hats and noise makers and ring in the new year.

How do you celebrate New Year's Eve? Are you one of the thousands of people standing in Times Square as the clock strikes 12:00?

Many people like watching the parades and bowl games on New Year's Day. Was your favorite team invited to play in one of the games? Were you fortunate enough to be there in person?

New Year's resolutions are another tradition. It doesn't matter whether you keep them or not, it's just fun to remember what they were. Jot them down!

New Year's Eve/Day

YEAR _____

EVE
Location: _____ Others Present
Activities & Traditions Observed: _____
_____
_____
_____
_____
_____
_____
_____

Additional Remarks: _____
_____

DAY
Location: _____ Others Present
Activities & Traditions Observed: _____
_____
_____
_____
_____
_____
_____
_____

Additional Remarks: _____
_____

Resolutions: _____
_____

YEAR _____

EVE
Location: _____ Others Present
Activities & Traditions Observed: _____
_____
_____

New Year's Eve/Day

Additional Remarks:

DAY

Location:

Activities & Traditions Observed:

Others Present

Additional Remarks:

Resolutions:

YEAR ____

EVE

Location:

Activities & Traditions Observed:

Others Present

Additional Remarks:

New Year's Eve/Day

DAY

Location: _____ Others Present

Activities & Traditions Observed: _____

_____

_____

_____

_____

_____

_____

Additional Remarks: _____

Resolutions: _____

YEAR _____

EVE

Location: _____ Others Present

Activities & Traditions Observed: _____

_____

_____

_____

_____

_____

_____

Additional Remarks: _____

DAY

Location: _____ Others Present

Activities & Traditions Observed: _____

_____

_____

New Year's Eve/Day

Additional Remarks: _____

Resolutions: _____

YEAR _____

EVE
Location: _____ Others Present
Activities & Traditions Observed: _____

Additional Remarks: _____

DAY
Location: _____ Others Present
Activities & Traditions Observed: _____

Additional Remarks: _____

Resolutions: _____

EASTER

YEAR _____

Location: _____ Others Present

Activities & Traditions Observed: _____ _____

_____ _____
_____ _____
_____ _____
_____ _____
_____ _____
_____ _____
_____ _____

Additional Remarks: _____
_____
_____

YEAR _____

Location: _____ Others Present

Activities & Traditions Observed: _____ _____

_____ _____
_____ _____
_____ _____
_____ _____
_____ _____
_____ _____
_____ _____

Additional Remarks: _____
_____
_____

YEAR _____

Location: _____ Others Present

Activities & Traditions Observed: _____ _____

_____ _____
_____ _____
_____ _____

Easter

Additional Remarks: _____

YEAR ____

Location: _____ Others Present
Activities & Traditions Observed: _____

Additional Remarks: _____

YEAR ____

Location: _____ Others Present
Activities & Traditions Observed: _____

Additional Remarks: _____

MEMORIAL DAY

YEAR _____

Location: _____   Others Present

Activities & Traditions Observed: _____   _____

_____   _____
_____   _____
_____   _____
_____   _____
_____   _____
_____   _____

Additional Remarks: _____

_____
_____

YEAR _____

Location: _____   Others Present

Activities & Traditions Observed: _____   _____

_____   _____
_____   _____
_____   _____
_____   _____
_____   _____
_____   _____

Additional Remarks: _____

_____
_____

YEAR _____

Location: _____   Others Present

Activities & Traditions Observed: _____   _____

_____   _____
_____   _____
_____   _____

Memorial Day

Additional Remarks:

YEAR

Location:
Activities & Traditions Observed:

Others Present

Additional Remarks:

YEAR

Location:
Activities & Traditions Observed:

Others Present

Additional Remarks:

Independence Day

YEAR _____

Location: _____ Others Present

Activities & Traditions Observed: _____

_____
_____
_____
_____
_____
_____
_____

Additional Remarks: _____

_____
_____

YEAR _____

Location: _____ Others Present

Activities & Traditions Observed: _____

_____
_____
_____
_____
_____
_____
_____

Additional Remarks: _____

_____
_____

YEAR _____

Location: _____ Others Present

Activities & Traditions Observed: _____

_____
_____
_____

# Independence Day

Additional Remarks:

YEAR

Location:
Activities & Traditions Observed:

Others Present

Additional Remarks:

YEAR

Location:
Activities & Traditions Observed:

Others Present

Additional Remarks:

Labor Day

YEAR _____

Location: _____   Others Present

Activities & Traditions Observed: _____   _____

_____   _____
_____   _____
_____   _____
_____   _____
_____   _____
_____   _____

Additional Remarks: _____
_____
_____

YEAR _____

Location: _____   Others Present

Activities & Traditions Observed: _____   _____

_____   _____
_____   _____
_____   _____
_____   _____
_____   _____
_____   _____

Additional Remarks: _____
_____
_____

YEAR _____

Location: _____   Others Present

Activities & Traditions Observed: _____   _____

_____   _____
_____   _____

LABOR DAY

Additional Remarks:

YEAR

Location:

Activities & Traditions Observed:

Others Present

Additional Remarks:

YEAR

Location:

Activities & Traditions Observed:

Others Present

Additional Remarks:

Thanksgiving

For many people, Thanksgiving marks the beginning of the holiday season and the gathering of relatives and friends for the traditional turkey dinner. Whether you continue to follow this tradition or have your own way of celebrating, Thanksgiving is always a holiday to remember.

Perhaps it's the baby's first Thanksgiving, or the first time in a long time all the adult children are home together. What special meals and wine did you enjoy? Is there a toast you want to remember? Did you go somewhere or do something worth noting?

Use the following pages to record the highlights of your Thanksgiving celebration.

THANKSGIVING

YEAR _____

Location: _____

Weather: _____

Travel Arrangements: _____

Others Present
_____

Activities & Traditions Observed: _____

Special Meals & Recipes

Additional Remarks: _____

THANKSGIVING

YEAR _____

Location: _____

Weather: _____

Travel Arrangements: _____

_____

_____

_____

_____

_____

_____

_____

_____

Others Present

_____

_____

_____

_____

_____

_____

_____

_____

_____

_____

Activities & Traditions Observed: _____

_____

_____

_____

_____

_____

_____

_____

_____

_____

_____

_____

_____

Special Meals & Recipes

_____

_____

_____

_____

_____

_____

_____

_____

_____

_____

_____

_____

_____

Additional Remarks: _____

_____

_____

_____

_____

_____

THANKSGIVING

YEAR _____

Location: _____
Weather: _____
Travel Arrangements: _____

Others Present
_____

Activities & Traditions Observed: _____

Special Meals & Recipes
_____

Additional Remarks: _____

THANKSGIVING

YEAR _____

Location: _____

Weather: _____

Travel Arrangements: _____

Others Present
_____
_____
_____
_____
_____
_____
_____
_____
_____
_____

Activities & Traditions Observed: _____

Special Meals & Recipes

Additional Remarks: _____

THANKSGIVING

YEAR _____

Location: _____

Weather: _____

Travel Arrangements: _____

Others Present
_____

Activities & Traditions Observed: _____

Special Meals & Recipes
_____

Additional Remarks: _____

Christmas Eve/Day

Christmas season is the highlight of the year for many families. You can easily fill up several pages with your Christmas memories of presents under the tree, gatherings of family and friends, parties, toasts, traditional meals, and special treats.

Many families have different activities occurring on Christmas Eve and Christmas Day, as well as the whole week, so you may want to record a great deal of information. Decide what you especially want to remember and describe it on the following yearly pages.

If you exchange gifts outside of your immediate family, e.g. with your brother's or sister's family, then you can record the gifts you purchased for them under Gifts Given, and the gifts your family received under Gifts Received.

If there is more information than space available, be selective and note only very special gifts and moments, or use the Additional Remarks page at the end of this chapter.

In addition to preserving cherished memories, the gift information you record can help prevent giving duplicate gifts in the future.

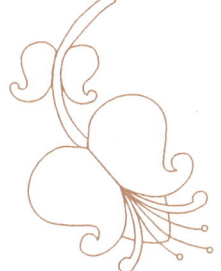

Christmas Eve

YEAR _____

Location: _____

Weather: _____

Travel Arrangements: _____

Special Meals & Recipes
_____

Others Present
_____

Activities & Traditions Observed: _____

Gifts Given

Given By	Given To	Gifts

Christmas Day

YEAR _____

Location: _____

Weather: _____

Travel Arrangements: _____

Special Meals & Recipes
_____
_____
_____
_____
_____
_____

Others Present
_____
_____
_____
_____
_____
_____

Activities & Traditions Observed: _____
_____
_____
_____
_____
_____
_____
_____
_____

Gifts Received

Given By	Given To	Gifts

Christmas Eve

YEAR _____

Location: _____

Weather: _____

Travel Arrangements: _____

Special Meals & Recipes
_____
_____
_____
_____
_____
_____
_____

Others Present
_____
_____
_____
_____
_____
_____
_____

Activities & Traditions Observed: _____
_____
_____
_____
_____
_____
_____
_____
_____
_____

Gifts Given

Given By	Given To	Gifts

Christmas Day

YEAR _____

Location: _____

Weather: _____

Travel Arrangements: _____

Special Meals & Recipes
_____
_____
_____
_____
_____
_____

Others Present
_____
_____
_____
_____
_____
_____

Activities & Traditions Observed: _____
_____
_____
_____
_____
_____
_____
_____

Gifts Received

Given By	Given To	Gifts

Christmas Eve

YEAR _____

Location: _____

Weather: _____

Travel Arrangements: _____
_____
_____

Special Meals & Recipes
_____
_____
_____
_____
_____
_____

Others Present
_____
_____
_____
_____
_____
_____

Activities & Traditions Observed: _____
_____
_____
_____
_____
_____
_____
_____

Gifts Given

Given By	Given To	Gifts

Christmas Day

YEAR _____

Location: _____

Weather: _____

Travel Arrangements: _____

Special Meals & Recipes
_____

Others Present
_____

Activities & Traditions Observed: _____
_____
_____
_____
_____
_____
_____

Gifts Received

Given By	Given To	Gifts

Christmas Eve

YEAR _____

Location: _____

Weather: _____

Travel Arrangements: _____

Special Meals & Recipes
_____
_____
_____
_____
_____
_____

Others Present
_____
_____
_____
_____
_____
_____

Activities & Traditions Observed: _____
_____
_____
_____
_____
_____
_____
_____
_____

Gifts Given

Given By	Given To	Gifts

CHRISTMAS DAY

YEAR _____

Location: _____

Weather: _____

Travel Arrangements: _____

Special Meals & Recipes

Others Present

Activities & Traditions Observed: _____

Gifts Received

Given By	Given To	Gifts

Christmas Eve

YEAR _____

Location: _____

Weather: _____

Travel Arrangements: _____

Special Meals & Recipes
_____
_____
_____
_____
_____
_____
_____

Others Present
_____
_____
_____
_____
_____
_____
_____

Activities & Traditions Observed: _____
_____
_____
_____
_____
_____
_____
_____
_____

Gifts Given

Given By	Given To	Gifts

Christmas Day

YEAR _____

Location: _____

Weather: _____

Travel Arrangements: _____

Special Meals & Recipes

Others Present

Activities & Traditions Observed: _____

Gifts Received

Given By	Given To	Gifts

Christmas
Additional Remarks

YEAR _____

YEAR _____

YEAR _____

YEAR _____

YEAR _____

Birthdays

For children—and for many adults—birthdays are very important.

On the following pages you will find room for recording those days of special recognition for all members of your family. What presents were received? From whom? Was there a party or other observance to mark the day?

If you keep a short record for each year, you will be able to look back and see which types of birthday celebrations you want to repeat. You can also see which gifts were received and avoid giving a duplicate gift later.

If you need more room for recording the birthday celebrations of people outside your immediate family—aunts, uncles, grandparents and cousins—use the Additional Remarks page at the end of this chapter.

Have a Happy Birthday!

BIRTHDAYS

YEAR _____

Name	Age	How Celebrated	Gifts	Given By

BIRTHDAYS

YEAR _____

Name	Age	How Celebrated	Gifts	Given By

BIRTHDAYS

YEAR _____

Name	Age	How Celebrated	Gifts	Given By

BIRTHDAYS

YEAR _____

Name	Age	How Celebrated	Gifts	Given By

BIRTHDAYS

YEAR _____

Name	Age	How Celebrated	Gifts	Given By

Birthdays
Additional Remarks

YEAR _____

YEAR _____

YEAR _____

YEAR _____

YEAR _____

Guests & Visitors

If you have moved away from family and friends, you may have had the joy of having those special people visit your new home.

On the following pages you can record who visited you and when they came. Whether you gave the "grand tour" of the major attractions in your city, sat up all night catching up on news about old acquaintances, or just provided comfortable accommodations for friends traveling through town, you will enjoy reading a brief description of these visits years from now.

Guests & Visitors

Dates	Guests/Visitors	Activities

Guests & Visitors

Dates	Guests/Visitors	Activities

Guests & Visitors

Dates	Guests/Visitors	Activities

Milestones

If you are already using any of the scrapbooks, photo albums, and baby books available for recording each family member's activities, the following pages for brief summaries will complement those records very well.

Record your children's activities and achievements in school, scouts, 4-H, sports, music, dance, and camp. This is also a good place to record graduations.

Don't forget to include your own professional honors, degrees earned, and civic awards!

What fun it will be, years from now, for you and the children to look back at these yearly highlights!

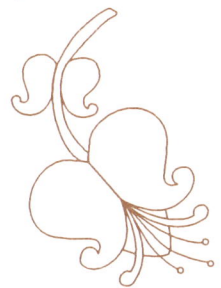

MILESTONES

YEAR _____

Name	Age	Activities, Achievements, Events

Milestones

YEAR _____

Name	Age	Activities, Achievements, Events

MILESTONES

YEAR _____

Name	Age	Activities, Achievements, Events

MILESTONES

YEAR _____

| Name | Age | Activities, Achievements, Events |

Milestones

YEAR _____

Name	Age	Activities, Achievements, Events

MILESTONES
ADDITIONAL REMARKS

YEAR _____

YEAR _____

YEAR _____

YEAR _____

YEAR _____

Odds & Ends

Many miscellaneous events, accomplishments, and changes that occur in each year can be recorded on the following pages. For example, there are special sections for recording births, weddings, and deaths of friends and relatives.

Under Health Notes, record that first pair of glasses, a broken leg while skiing, first (or last!) gray hair, mammograms, dental braces and crowns, or hospital stays.

Was this the year you finally got to remodel your kitchen or build that deck you always wanted? Did you purchase a new television, VCR, or boat? If so, record them in the Major Purchases/Home Improvements section.

Current Events lets you tie significant local or international events to the significant events in your life. Perhaps this was the year you experienced "The Storm of the Century."

The category entitled "Other" would be a good place to record the day you started building or actually moved into your "dream home." You could also use this section for noting any investments, special conferences attended, the meeting of someone famous, winning a special prize or award, the completion of a special project, or the inheritance of a vast fortune (you never know!)

Odds & Ends

YEAR _____

Births	Weddings	Deaths
_____	_____	_____
_____	_____	_____
_____	_____	_____
_____	_____	_____

Job Changes: _____

Residence Changes: _____

School Changes: _____
Major Purchases/Home Improvements: _____

Health Notes: _____

Current Events: _____

Other: _____

Odds & Ends

YEAR _____

Births	Weddings	Deaths
_____	_____	_____
_____	_____	_____
_____	_____	_____
_____	_____	_____

Job Changes: _____

Residence Changes: _____

School Changes: _____
Major Purchases/Home Improvements: __

Health Notes: _____

Current Events: _____

Other: _____

Odds & Ends

YEAR ____

Births	Weddings	Deaths
_____	_____	_____
_____	_____	_____
_____	_____	_____
_____	_____	_____

Job Changes: _____

Residence Changes: _____

School Changes: _____

Major Purchases/Home Improvements: _____

Health Notes: _____

Current Events: _____

Other: _____

Odds & Ends

YEAR _____

Births	Weddings	Deaths

Job Changes: _____

Residence Changes: _____

School Changes: _____
Major Purchases/Home Improvements: _____

Health Notes: _____

Current Events: _____

Other: _____

Odds & Ends

YEAR _____

Births	Weddings	Deaths
_____	_____	_____
_____	_____	_____
_____	_____	_____
_____	_____	_____

Job Changes: _____

Residence Changes: _____

School Changes: _____
Major Purchases/Home Improvements: _____

Health Notes: _____

Current Events: _____

Other: _____

Parties & Informal Gatherings

Parties are special events, whether they are intimate dinner parties or an informal gathering of neighbors for a barbecue or block party.

If you enjoy parties, you now have a place to keep a summary of the details. The information you record will be fun to look back at and come in handy when you are planning to host a future gathering or merely attend one.

If there was a particular theme to the gathering, a special reason for celebrating, or an exceptional menu or recipe, you can note this information for easy reference. There is also room for recording the names of guests and any reflections you had after the party.

Parties & Informal Gatherings

Date: _____

Location: _____

Type of Gathering: _____

Special Meals & Recipes: _____

Others Present: _____

Activities & Highlights: _____

Date: _____

Location: _____

Type of Gathering: _____

Special Meals & Recipes: _____

Others Present: _____

Activities & Highlights: _____

Date: _____

Location: _____

Type of Gathering: _____

Special Meals & Recipes: _____

Others Present: _____

Activities & Highlights: _____

Date: _____

Location: _____

Type of Gathering: _____

Special Meals & Recipes: _____

Others Present: _____

Activities & Highlights: _____

Parties & Informal Gatherings

	Special Meals & Recipes	Others Present
Date: _____	_____	_____
Location: _____	_____	_____
Type of Gathering: _____	_____	_____

Activities & Highlights: _____

_____

	Special Meals & Recipes	Others Present
Date: _____	_____	_____
Location: _____	_____	_____
Type of Gathering: _____	_____	_____

Activities & Highlights: _____

_____

	Special Meals & Recipes	Others Present
Date: _____	_____	_____
Location: _____	_____	_____
Type of Gathering: _____	_____	_____

Activities & Highlights: _____

_____

	Special Meals & Recipes	Others Present
Date: _____	_____	_____
Location: _____	_____	_____
Type of Gathering: _____	_____	_____

Activities & Highlights: _____

_____

Parties & Informal Gatherings

	Special Meals & Recipes	Others Present
Date:		
Location:		
Type of Gathering:		

Activities & Highlights:

	Special Meals & Recipes	Others Present
Date:		
Location:		
Type of Gathering:		

Activities & Highlights:

	Special Meals & Recipes	Others Present
Date:		
Location:		
Type of Gathering:		

Activities & Highlights:

	Special Meals & Recipes	Others Present
Date:		
Location:		
Type of Gathering:		

Activities & Highlights:

Parties & Informal Gatherings

	Special Meals & Recipes	Others Present
Date:		
Location:		
Type of Gathering:		

Activities & Highlights: _____

	Special Meals & Recipes	Others Present
Date:		
Location:		
Type of Gathering:		

Activities & Highlights: _____

	Special Meals & Recipes	Others Present
Date:		
Location:		
Type of Gathering:		

Activities & Highlights: _____

	Special Meals & Recipes	Others Present
Date:		
Location:		
Type of Gathering:		

Activities & Highlights: _____

Parties & Informal Gatherings

Date: _____

   Location: _____
   Type of Gathering: _____

   Activities & Highlights: _____

Special Meals & Recipes
_____
_____
_____
_____

Others Present
_____
_____
_____
_____

Date: _____

   Location: _____
   Type of Gathering: _____

   Activities & Highlights: _____

Special Meals & Recipes
_____
_____
_____
_____

Others Present
_____
_____
_____
_____

Date: _____

   Location: _____
   Type of Gathering: _____

   Activities & Highlights: _____

Special Meals & Recipes
_____
_____
_____
_____

Others Present
_____
_____
_____
_____

Date: _____

   Location: _____
   Type of Gathering: _____

   Activities & Highlights: _____

Special Meals & Recipes
_____
_____
_____
_____

Others Present
_____
_____
_____
_____

Parties & Informal Gatherings

Date: _____

   Location: _____

   Type of Gathering: _____

Special Meals & Recipes
_____
_____
_____
_____

Others Present
_____
_____
_____
_____

Activities & Highlights: _____
_____
_____

Date: _____

   Location: _____

   Type of Gathering: _____

Special Meals & Recipes
_____
_____
_____
_____

Others Present
_____
_____
_____
_____

Activities & Highlights: _____
_____
_____

Date: _____

   Location: _____

   Type of Gathering: _____

Special Meals & Recipes
_____
_____
_____
_____

Others Present
_____
_____
_____
_____

Activities & Highlights: _____
_____
_____

Date: _____

   Location: _____

   Type of Gathering: _____

Special Meals & Recipes
_____
_____
_____
_____

Others Present
_____
_____
_____
_____

Activities & Highlights: _____
_____
_____

Parties & Informal Gatherings
Additional Remarks

DATE _____ _____

_____
_____
_____
_____
_____

DATE _____ _____

_____
_____
_____
_____
_____

DATE _____ _____

_____
_____
_____
_____
_____

DATE _____ _____

_____
_____
_____
_____
_____

DATE _____ _____

_____
_____
_____
_____
_____

Reunions

They say that class reunions are the leading cause of weight loss in the country. In spite of the pre-reunion anxiety, most people have a marvelous time.

Here is a great place to record the highlights of your reunion including who you saw, how they looked, and what favorite stories were relived.

Whether it's a high school, military, church, or family reunion, reading the highlights years from now will certainly put a smile on your face.

If there is not enough room for recording all the information you want, use the Additional Remarks page at the end of this chapter.

Reunions

Date: _____ Location: _____ Others Present
Type of Reunion: _____ _____
Activities & Highlights: _____ _____
_____ _____
_____ _____
_____ _____
_____ _____
_____ _____
_____ _____
_____ _____
_____ _____
_____ _____
_____ _____
_____ _____
_____ _____
_____ _____
_____ _____
_____ _____
_____ _____
_____ _____
_____ _____
_____ _____
_____ _____

Date: _____ Location: _____ Others Present
Type of Reunion: _____ _____
Activities & Highlights: _____ _____
_____ _____
_____ _____
_____ _____
_____ _____
_____ _____
_____ _____
_____ _____

REUNIONS

Date: _____ Location: _____
Type of Reunion: _____
Activities & Highlights: _____

Others Present

Reunions
Additional Remarks

DATE _____ _____

DATE _____ _____

DATE _____ _____

Special Celebrations

Every family celebrates many different holidays and events. Since there is not enough room to include all holidays individually, this section is provided so you can record the special days and occasions specific to your family.

Special Celebrations can include events such as Hanukkah, Passover, Mother's Day, Father's Day, Bar Mitzvahs, Confirmations, Baptisms, graduations, and open houses.

This is also the place for recording that nice gift you received on Secretary's or Boss' Day, a unique Valentine's Day present, a St. Patrick's Day party, Oktoberfest, or your favorite team making the Superbowl or World Series.

Decide which holidays and happenings you want to remember and include them on the following yearly pages. This is a good place to include all those miscellaneous events and activities you don't want to forget.

Special Celebrations

Date | Special Celebrations

Special Celebrations

Date	Special Celebrations

Special Celebrations

Date   Special Celebrations

Special Celebrations

Date	Special Celebrations

Special Celebrations

Date Special Celebrations

Trips & Vacations

Getting away from it all often means traveling to different and interesting places where you can relax, see new sights, and meet new people.

Was this the year the family took the Colorado River raft trip? What about a luxurious cruise to the Virgin Islands? Did you take part in a volunteer service trip helping researchers dig for artifacts in Mexico?

While traveling miles from home, did you meet some "new" people who turned out to be neighbors on your street or from your old home town? Often the things you do and the people you meet are more memorable than the actual site of the vacation.

Be sure to write down the name of that favorite, romantic bistro or out-of-the-way village you visited so that you can refer it to friends or return there yourself.

Your vacation notes and specific references can help you, in years to come, relive those pleasant and stimulating experiences.

Trips & Vacations

Date & Occasion: _____
    Family/Friends: _____
    Places Visited: _____
_____

Highlights: _____
_____
_____
_____

Date & Occasion: _____
    Family/Friends: _____
    Places Visited: _____
_____

Highlights: _____
_____
_____
_____

Date & Occasion: _____
    Family/Friends: _____
    Places Visited: _____
_____

Highlights: _____
_____
_____
_____

Date & Occasion: _____
    Family/Friends: _____
    Places Visited: _____
_____

Highlights: _____
_____
_____
_____

Trips & Vacations

Date & Occasion: _____
   Family/Friends: _____
   Places Visited: _____
_____

Highlights: _____
_____
_____
_____

Date & Occasion: _____
   Family/Friends: _____
   Places Visited: _____
_____

Highlights: _____
_____
_____
_____

Date & Occasion: _____
   Family/Friends: _____
   Places Visited: _____
_____

Highlights: _____
_____
_____
_____

Date & Occasion: _____
   Family/Friends: _____
   Places Visited: _____
_____

Highlights: _____
_____
_____
_____

Trips & Vacations

Date & Occasion: _____
    Family/Friends: _____
    Places Visited: _____
_____

Highlights: _____
_____
_____
_____

Date & Occasion: _____
    Family/Friends: _____
    Places Visited: _____
_____

Highlights: _____
_____
_____
_____

Date & Occasion: _____
    Family/Friends: _____
    Places Visited: _____
_____

Highlights: _____
_____
_____
_____

Date & Occasion: _____
    Family/Friends: _____
    Places Visited: _____
_____

Highlights: _____
_____
_____
_____

Trips & Vacations

Date & Occasion: _____
   Family/Friends: _____
   Places Visited: _____
_____
Highlights: _____
_____
_____
_____

Date & Occasion: _____
   Family/Friends: _____
   Places Visited: _____
_____
Highlights: _____
_____
_____
_____

Date & Occasion: _____
   Family/Friends: _____
   Places Visited: _____
_____
Highlights: _____
_____
_____
_____

Date & Occasion: _____
   Family/Friends: _____
   Places Visited: _____
_____
Highlights: _____
_____
_____
_____

Trips & Vacations

Date & Occasion: _____
    Family/Friends: _____
    Places Visited: _____
_____

Highlights: _____
_____
_____
_____

Date & Occasion: _____
    Family/Friends: _____
    Places Visited: _____
_____

Highlights: _____
_____
_____
_____

Date & Occasion: _____
    Family/Friends: _____
    Places Visited: _____
_____

Highlights: _____
_____
_____
_____

Date & Occasion: _____
    Family/Friends: _____
    Places Visited: _____
_____

Highlights: _____
_____
_____
_____

Wedding Anniversaries

Sometimes memories of those years between the major anniversaries (e.g. Silver, Golden) have a way of becoming lost.

If you want to remember what you did on every anniversary—whether you spent a quiet evening at home together, had a romantic candlelight dinner for two, or went on an exotic cruise—you can summarize the major details in this chapter.

The following pages will serve to commemorate and preserve the beautiful anniversaries of your marriage.

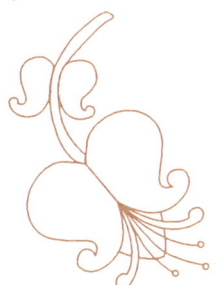

Wedding Anniversaries

Year	Years Married	How Celebrated	Gifts	Given By

Wedding Anniversaries
Additional Remarks

YEAR _____

YEAR _____

YEAR _____

YEAR _____

YEAR _____

Extra Notes

Extra Notes